To Hilary
best wishes

Kawasaki

The Promise

This book does not require any previous knowledge of Zen to be enjoyable, any more than it requires the reader to be a golfer.

Having said that, here is the promise: Any committed player, no matter what their handicap ~ from novice to master ~ all can benefit and improve their game ~ whatever game they play on the fairway of life ~ by the simple application of Zen.

This book shows you how.

Zen
and the art of
Golf

A sure way to improve your game

by

Yoshi Kawasaki

• Ian Hunter Publications •

Published in 1998 by
IAN HUNTER PUBLICATIONS
68-74 King Street
Norwich, Norfolk, NR1 1PG

ISBN 0 9534189 0 1

Cover design and typesetting by Andrew Larkin
Typeset in Bembo 12/14pt

For Mike Sowerby
Paterfamilias and golfer extraordinaire.

Zen
and the art of
Golf

"What is Zen?" a pupil asked.
Mumon replied, "Zen aims through meditation to realise the emancipation of one's mind. It offers a method of self searching usually under the personal guidance of a master.
What a joke!"

Ekai, called Mumon (d.1228)★.

★*Unless otherwise stated, all dates given are AD.*

1

There was no bell.

Jones took a coin from his pocket and rapped on the door.

The girl who opened to him was a shock to the system: un-nervingly lovely, with the high cheek bones and slanting cat eyes of the Oriental. But she was tall for a Chinese, flat-chested, with no hips worth talking about, her age impossible to guess at. Thirteen or thirty? Anything.

There was one thing though, that distinguished her, that marked her out ~ quite literally ~ from the ranks of the conventionally beautiful. Her birthmark. Africa-shaped and alizarin red, it dominated but failed, sublimely, to disfigure the lefthand side of her face.

"Excuse me, I'm looking for a Mr. Ah Toy."

"Wait please."

The door was closed in his face ~ not rudely ~ an inch being left ajar. A pause. The sound of voices; an un-intelligible language. Again the door opened, the red-stained Lynx making a welcome reappearance.

"Come in please."

What is Zen?
"Those who know do not speak
Those who speak do not know."

Lao-tzu (d.479 BC).

2

The room he was shown into displayed all the comforts of a hermit's cell: un-carpeted floor, no ornaments, and no pictures to brighten the bare walls; only three clocks, each showing a different time. And there was little in the way of furniture: a couch, that probably did service as a bed, a ricepaper screen masking off an open door and two ancient upholstered chairs set near an open window ~ the coffee table between them bearing a full ashtray.

In one of the ancient chairs sat an old Chinaman, very old, very frail, his silver hair cropped to a stubble and wearing small round gold-rimmed spectacles. He did not rise in greeting and it was only when Jones moved across the room to face him, that he noticed the walking frame.

"Mr. Toy? I'm looking for Mr. Jimmy Ah Toy."

"You have found him. Sit please."

"Ah! Sir, I understand that you are a Zen master."

Silence.

Jones was not entirely fazed by this. He had read often enough that Zen can not be communicated by words, that to speak of Zen is futile. Silence, then, is not totally inappropriate; a means of communication even. But this was not likely to get him very far.

He tried again.

"Sir, I seek a master."

Again there was no reply, the only sound in the room, the ceiling fan's helicopter flutter and the distant drone of traffic seeping through the open window.

Jones could not now speak further; he had made his petition and there was no room here for prevarication. The ball was firmly in the other's court.

Ten minutes went by. Jones could accurately gauge time's passing by following the minute hand on the wallclock opposite; a clock of the gilt sunburst variety ~ a clock which he would get to know well during the weeks to come.

Surprisingly, the supplicant found that he was not overly distressed by this long silence. He had made his request and there was nothing more to be said or done. Except wait. He was relaxed, at ease almost, feeling in some odd way removed from himself; a spectator rather than a participant.

"At least you're not a chatterbox." Toy finally spoke. "Come back tomorrow."

Jones stood, inclined his head in a token bow and left, seeing himself out.

Hell! That was going to be awkward. Two meetings would have to be cancelled... No! Delegate. Make young Robson work for his money. This was important.

"Thank you for smoking.
Anyone caught not smoking on these premises may be asked to leave."

Sign in a tobacconist's window ~ Cromer.

3

The next day was a carbon copy of the first. The girl, the room, the old man, all were exactly as before. Exactly. It was a trifle disconcerting, as if nothing really had moved or altered during the intervening twenty four hours; even the stubs in the ashtray looked the same.

Toy indicated that Jones should sit. He sat. In silence. A full twenty minutes of it this time.

Jesus! this old Chinaman was making life difficult. But Jones was aware that this was some kind of test; a test of his stamina, perhaps, or of his earnestness. He didn't know how well he was doing, though, or how much longer he would be expected to 'play'. Weeks? If need be, he would. In any event, there was always the pleasurable shock of the girl to look forward to...

What is Zen?
"Lighting flashes,
Sparks shower.
In one blink of your eyes
You have missed seeing."

(Mumon).

4

Day three was more of the same. Jones was resigned to it by now, his initial irritation having long since evaporated. He had no doubts at all, none, that Toy was the master that he sought, and like a good neophyte, he did not question his master's wisdom ~ or his continued silence.

In fact there was a quietude here, a peacefulness, that Jones had rarely met with in the distractions of his daily life. He had come to welcome these silent afternoons.

A fly buzzed against the window pane, vainly seeking an exit. Buzz, buzz. Rest. Then buzz, buzz, a repeat performance, over and over; completely futile. Yet, less than a foot below was the wide-open world. So close. But the insect, having learnt nothing, would die on that ledge, its bristly little body dried out and lifeless.

Toy knew about the fly. He knew everything that happened in this still room. It was a message, a lesson, Jones could sense it. But what about the girl, where did she fit in? And in a flash it was all lost.

Everything. All that was beginning to come so clear ~ through the effort of a fly ~ all lost. The girl... Thoughts, aimless thoughts sliding and slipping over one another, coruscating in the mind's eye...

"Come again tomorrow."

The time had slipped away.

Outside on the landing Jones checked his watch. Nearly half an hour! Incredible.

"What is Zen?" a monk asked Fuketsu.
"Without speaking, without silence, how can you express the truth?"
Answer: "If you want to express the truth, throw out your words,
throw out your silence and tell me about your own Zen."

Mumon.

5

Day four. Again, the girl to open the door and again, the changeless timeless room. Yet, on this occasion, Jones sensed something different: there was a subtle fragrance in the air. On the table between the two chairs stood a small vase, with a spray of some unknown white-petalled flowers.

"Sit." (No 'please' this time.)

"You show persistence. Coming like this at my beck and call must surely inconvenience you?"

At last a chance to speak.

"No Sir, it does not inconvenience me, only my work is inconvenienced, and that only slightly. I have re-scheduled my day and handed over more responsibility to my assistant; something I should have done long ago. In fact ~ when I think about it ~ I'd say that the business has improved rather than suffered by this new arrangement." Jones hesitated, on the brink... "and I get to play more golf."

The cropped head nodded slightly. It seemed to have been a satisfactory reply. But the clear old eyes were difficult to read behind their heavy lenses and the mouth was unsmiling too. Yet it was not an unkind mouth, just a thin-lipped seam expressing nothing, a horizontal suture in a skein of lines and wrinkles. Finding a grain of encouragement in this Jones stumbled on:

"I seek to improve myself."

"What is it that you seek to improve?"

Coming abruptly like this, the blunt question took Jones by surprise and he answered directly.

"My golf. I need to improve my golf, my proficiency, my ~ my enjoyment."

There was a sharp barking sound from the Chinaman ~ "Bwah!" might come close to it ~ and then Jones was further astonished to see that the old man was laughing, laughing fit to burst, the frail old body shaking with silent laughter.

It took some time for Toy to recover. He removed his spectacles, wiping at his eyes with a pocket handkerchief.

"Thank you. I am indebted to you for your teaching. But you look pained. You are shocked at my finding your obsession amusing?"

In the lack of a reply, the old man continued.

"No, I think not. You are dismayed at my having laughed. A master should be above such things. Eh? Isn't that it?" He leaned forward.

"Well, let me tell you a great secret. I am as human as you are. Yes, I piss and I shit just like you do, and if God chooses to give me the equipment for laughter then why should I spurn his great gift?"

Jones was listening open-mouthed. The Chinaman had not only accurately read his thoughts, he was giving them substance.

"Well? Am I wiser than my maker? Do I know something he doesn't? An arcane knowledge, perhaps, passed down from master to pupil from the days of the Buddha?"

There was more than just a hint of irony in Toy's voice. He lit a cigarette, blowing out smoke, fixing Jones with his eyes.

"I will take you as a pupil. Do you agree to serve?"

"Yes Sir." Jones was overjoyed. "When shall we begin?"

"Begin! We have been at work for four days now."

A pause. Toy spoke again.

"You have not mentioned yet what you will pay me for my teaching."

"No Sir, I felt ~ I still feel ~ that speaking of money would be inappropriate, insulting, perhaps. What you have to offer can not, surely, be purchased but only offered freely, as a gift."

"Yes, I guessed so. You will make a good pupil; you are quick and open to learning."

Toy looked away, eyes unfocused, stubbing out his cigarette and absently lighting another.

"In payment, will you build me a temple?" he asked.

"Yes Sir."

"But you are not a wealthy man."

"No Sir."

"Then how will you build it?"

"I will find the money." Jones answered directly, without taking pause for thought. "It will be built, no matter what the cost."

This seemed to please the old man, his face creased into a brief smile, showing stained yellow teeth.

"Good. There is your first lesson. Hold true to that: no matter what the cost, the temple must be built. Nothing less will do. I am not an arbiter in these matters. It is so."

Jones held his breath, too excited to speak. He had been accepted! But there was no more.

"Until tomorrow."

First Interlude

"Golf is the perfect paradigm for life."

Arnold Palmer in conversation with John Pratt.

Jones and Golf

Jones was an inveterate golfer. He loved golf. He loved everything about it: the anticipation, the game itself and the clubhouse afterwards. And no matter what the weather, no matter what the course, he would be out there playing. Or, if not actually playing, then wishing that he were. Only snow had been known to stop him, and here in Darwin, only nine hundred miles below the equator, the chances of that were astronomically remote.

Perversely, in the capital of Australia's Northern Territory, where daytime temperatures rarely drop below ninety degrees and where there is no rain at all for nine months of the year, there are two fine golf courses. One, thanks to constant watering and the hardy Buffalo grass is of the traditional fairway and green variety, while the other, set in the margins of the Airforce base, offers a different, more challenging kind of game ~ the course being made, for the most part, from the ochre-coloured rock-hard soil.

At either venue, anything further removed, both in distance and climate from St. Andrew's famous links could not possibly be imagined. Many a national champion has been unseated in Darwin match play, where a tolerance for the crippling heat and humidity can be more than compensation for a relative lack of talent.

Yes, Jones loved his golf. It was the major focus in his life and he made no apology for it, finding a good deal more in the game than the exercise or the opportunity for social intercourse. Even the pleasure of winning ~ sweet though it tasted ~ was far outweighed by something less tangible: the almost ecstatic, euphoric feeling he experienced when playing really well. For when he played well, something happened: he felt uplifted, taken out of himself.

"Happiness" does not adequately describe the feeling. It is something deeper, something impossible to properly define ~ more a quiet ringing joy, the joy of completeness, a silent vibrating fizzing kind of joy. A sense of being at one with the club, the ball and the distant pin; a knowing, beyond uncertainty, that the great arc of the perfect swing will unerringly take the ball toward the distant green.

Not many golfers will admit to this sensation. Not in public. In their own ears it sounds too close to mysticism and it would definitely be begging ridicule in any self-respecting clubhouse. But they have all known it, at least once, this feeling. Or, if they have not ~ yet ~ then that is why they are out there, swinging and chipping, wet or fine, in the knowledge, deep down, that the feeling is there to be had.

Jones had caught more than just a glimpse of this sensation. He had caught the vivid scent of it twice now and he wanted it again, this 'fix', this thrill of completeness, this sense of being a part of Totality. Of being God...

"Teaching? What teaching?
There is nothing to be taught.
No, really. Nothing.
Discover for yourself."

The Seventh Patriarch.

6

Jones had been visiting Toy, his new-found master, for five days now and apart from the perennial pleasure of seeing the girl and being allowed to sit, figuratively speaking, at the Old Man's feet, he didn't seem to have got very far. There had been little talk of golf and none at all when it came to ways of improving his game. He cautiously broached the subject:

"Should I continue playing whilst under your tuition?"

"Playing?" There was a genuine note of incomprehension in Toy's voice.

"Yes, playing golf. It might interfere ~ you know ~ old habits, that kind of thing..."

"Oh! Golf! Yes, continue playing by all means. Why not? For myself, I find little of interest in the game. I have never played; but my ancestors did. One, a master in the T'ang Dynasty was a champion, or he would have been if he had entered tournaments. In friendly games he was unbeatable; the very best of China fell to his enlightened game."

Jones was astonished. "Golf goes that far back? The T'ang Dynasty that's ~ what ~ twelve hundred years ago! I never knew golf was that old."

"Oh yes. Like chess, the roots of golf are lost in antiquity."

Jones was now more at ease with the Chinaman and could

speak freely. For Toy, it have never been otherwise. But now the old man surprised him.

"How often do you play?" he asked.

Jones answered promptly: "Two or three times during the week and twice at weekends."

"When are you due to play next, and where do you play?"

Jones found this sudden burst of interest most gratifying and in response, became almost garrulous.

"Tomorrow. Tomorrow morning. I play in the mornings now ~ my afternoons are taken up elsewhere."

A short pause. But there was no response to this weak attempt at humour and, slightly deflated, he finished more lamely.

"I'm a member of the RAAF Club."

"Good. Then tomorrow morning play on the Town's course. Mary will go with you; she is not only my legs, but outside this room she is my eyes as well."

Mary! So the sphinx had a name.

"And if you can" Toy added, "play a round on your own. Nine holes will be sufficient.

"I will see you on Thursday."

"The way forward is clear.
There are no gates or barriers except of one's own making.
Golf? Of course, a perfect way,
Like any other."

The Seventh Patriarch.

7

With Mary seated beside him in the car Jones could, for the first time, look at her feet. Big feet ~ for a girl ~ size seven or eight, casually shod in grubby white plimsolls.

The hearse-like silence that he had steeled himself for did not materialise. Instead, Mary proved a vivacious and delightful companion. The conversation flowed easily between them, both being careful not to establish a monopoly. Jones was only too sorry when they finally turned into the Club's car park.

"I will wait here until you are ready to begin", she said.

"Are you sure? You could sit in the clubhouse, have a lemonade or something. There wouldn't be any problem."

Distinctions of race were not a part of Darwin's social life; not in a town-sized city that boasted no less than fifty different nationalities among its all-Australian citizenry. In any event, the Chinese community were generally acknowledged to be the wealthiest ~ and the most influential.

It was not possible to play a round on his own. Because of the appaling heat, morning play was more popular than in the afternoon. But the professional soon found a pair who would let him tag along ~ so long as they weren't "slowed up". Jones produced his certificate of handicap and that put paid to any further objections. They were due to tee-off in twenty minutes.

He went to collect the girl. She was not in the car. Where was she! He couldn't keep these old rednecks waiting. Ah! There she was, coming over from the bushes. What a delightful gliding walk she had... Then, up close, the shock! As vivid and as sharp as on the very first day. Sitting in the car, seeing only her right profile, he had forgotten all about the birthmark ~ now he saw that she had tucked a spray of bougainvillaea behind her ear, a good match for her face's stain. She was breathtaking.

What his fellow golfers thought of this strange caddy (she insisted on carrying the clubs) Jones never found out. They never asked and, unusually for Australians, passed no comment ~ not in his hearing, anyway.

He played well. There had been no "illumination", true, but he'd not expected there to be, not on this occasion. He had simply played as best he could, not to impress the girl, but to show ~ for Toy's unseen benefit ~ the best that he could manage. And though clearly unfamiliar with the task, Mary made an adequate caddy, never once losing sight of the ball; even when Jones sliced really badly on the fourth, she had little trouble in finding it, hidden among the stems of a clump of ginger. But on the course she did not speak beyond necessity. There were no comments and no instructions. She simply observed. Closely.

All in all, a very pleasant morning. Jones managed to finish only one shot over par; he felt quite pleased with himself.

"Would you care for a drink, Mary? Or some lunch perhaps? I don't know what the food's like here but I expect it's manageable."

"No. Thank you. Take me home please. I have to prepare lunch for Uncle."

"You're Mr. Toy's niece then."

Jones had expected that she'd be a relative of some kind. He would have thought her a granddaughter if it were not for the disparity in their ages; she had the look of the Old Man about her.

"No. Not a niece. I just call him Uncle, it is easier to say than great grandfather." She laughed. "Uncle says, often, that he is not 'great' only very ordinary."

Good Lord! Jones made some rapid mental calculations. Yes, it was well within the bounds of possibility, provided that Mary's mother and grandmother both married before they were twenty ~ which was not an unreasonable requirement. Well, well... Jones wished he'd had the nerve to ask how old she was.

"Not for idle contemplation of yourself are you here,
not for brooding over devout sensations ~
no, for action you are here;
action, and action alone, determines your worth. "

Johann Gottlieb Fichte (1800).

8

The next day, at Toy's open doorway, he was treated to a swift shy smile.

"Good afternoon Mary."

"Good afternoon".

Then the door was closed behind him and she was gone, as noiseless as a wraith on her rubber-soled shoes.

Silence was again the order of the day. This was not what Jones had expected; he had come armed, anticipating questions, but his well-rehearsed replies were immediately made redundant.

Still, the time had not been entirely wasted. Far from it. The prospect of being questioned had forced him to think hard and long, on subjects that he thought he knew well, but which, on close inspection, were found not to be well-known at all. It had been something of an eye-opener. He had never before allowed himself the time for such concentrated self-searching and now, with all the time in the world, insight and understanding were coming at him pellmell.

Once again, though, observing Jones closely, the Chinaman was well ahead of him. After a long silence ~ though brief by previous standards ~ Toy stubbed out his cigarette and speaking more to the ashtray than to Jones, rather took him by surprise.

"You learned a lot, I think, through yesterday's game." It was not a question.

"Yes Sir, and you have put it correctly: I learned through the game, not by the playing."

"Good. You have a favourite club I believe."

"Yes Sir, I do. My putter. It was made specially for me by an Abbo Pro at a Club in Melbourne." Jones warmed to his subject. "It has an ironwood head and a carbon steel shaft. It fits me perfectly: just the right weight, in just the right place."

"So. But this perfect club, this ideal tool, it can still let you down?"

"Yes, often. But I think it's me that fails the club, not the other way around. I can improve myself, I hope, but not my old ironwood."

While Jones had been speaking Toy seemed to be taking more interest in the smoke coiling from his cigarette than in Jones' eulogy.

"Do you have it with you, this club? Is it in your car?"

"Yes."

"Go and fetch it will you, I'd like to see it."

Second Interlude

A bold monk once asked Ekai:
"Master, are you satisfied with your life?"
Answer: "At this moment, yes."
"But", the monk went on, "Are you happy ?"
Answer: "Happy enough."

The Seventh Patriarch.

A Brief History Of Golf

The German scholar Herbert Riedal assures us that golf was played in China more than a thousand years ago; there are pictures from the T'ang Dynasty (618-907) that clearly show elegantly dressed ladies addressing the ball. But it is more likely to have been an indoor or garden game rather than the cross-country outdoor variety that we have come to associate with the name.

The first indisputable reference to golf proper, appears in a Dutch manuscript of 1297. The game ~ colf ~ was popular in Holland, usually being played in the winter months, over frozen fields and lakes. There were no holes, and instead, targets were agreed on: a barn door, a particular tree, or a peg driven into the ice.

This continued well into the mid-eighteenth century when colf gave way to kolf, a game with a set course, holes (with flag markers) and rules, which were mainly borrowed from the Scots, who had been playing their own version of the game for centuries.

Scotland is the traditional home of golf ~ some say its birthplace ~ and it was certainly sufficiently popular by 1457 for King James II to issue a Royal Decree forbidding the playing of gowf (and futeball) on the grounds that it was interfering with the more practical business of archery practice.

Another factor, often overlooked, that aided in making golf a year-round activity was the invention of the mowing-machine, which made permanent fairways a practical proposition.

*"Of course, I still have that taste for disorder,
but now it's a more solitary affair."*

Jah Wobble from the CD 'Rising Above Bedlam'.

9

Toy held the putter in both hands, scrutinising it, observing closely how the head was grafted to the shank.

"Yes, a fine piece of work. Very well made. Mary!" he called.

When she appeared from behind the screen, he addressed her at length, in ~ presumably ~ Chinese. She left the room to return a moment later carrying a meatcleaver, its stainless-steel blade gleaming wickedly.

Jones felt the distinctive prickling of pure, unalloyed fear. Toy registered this and smiled reassuringly.

"This is not for you Mr. Jones but it is for you to use. Take it."

In shocked surprise, Jones obediently took the weapon from Mary's hands. It felt cold and heavy. Lethal.

Still sitting, Toy held the club in a firm two-handed grip with its wooden head facing upwards, resting on the floorboards.

"Now, strike at your club's face. Strike hard, with all your might. Destroy your club!"

Jones' trust held firm.

Dropping to one knee, at his master's feet, he lifted the cleaver, judged the distance and struck ~ hard ~ at the polished well-loved face. The bright steel flashed, embedding itself briefly in the ironwood, leaving a quarter-inch deep scar.

"There, you have killed your favourite tool. It is dead beyond resurrection."

Jones felt slightly ill and had to sit down again. Why? Why

should he have to 'kill' his favourite club? Where was the lesson?

Mary had taken away the cleaver along with the dead 'tool' and now she reappeared, eyes twinkling and grinning from ear to ear. So, she was behind all this... She carried a brand new golf club, a putter, a perfectly ordinary, perfectly adequate no-name putter ~ made in Japan. She gave it to Toy who, with an air of ceremony, offered it, two-handed, to Jones.

"Here is your new club, accept and honour it as a gift. Do not just tolerate it. There is no room for tolerance in golf, any more than there is in life."

Jones was non-plussed.

"But Sir, surely tolerance is a great virtue, one of the cornerstones of a civilised society."

Toy was unmoved.

"Where is this civilised society you speak of? Can you tell me? No, you can't. Humankind remain savages at heart, living in reaction to stimulus, like any other beast. Only the surface of things alters; rather than bother with a dish of whale-oil and a wick, we now turn on the electric light. That's all."

This was all very well, understandable, even. But what of tolerance?

"Should we be intolerant then?"

Toy was quick to reply, savagely grinding out his cigarette, irritation beginning to show in his voice.

"No, of course not. Intolerance is as stupid and as stultifying as its opposite. Listen! An American writer, Henry Miller, a man who truly possessed the Buddha nature, once wrote:

'*There is only one sin and that is weakness. Do not add your own weakness to the evil that is going to come. Be strong.*'

"Rather good, don't you think? Tolerance is nothing more

than a form of weakness ~ a cowardice, if you prefer. If you know something to be wrong and you tolerate it, then, by your silence ~ by your tolerance ~ you connive with the wrong and your silence lends it your approval.

"Either accept a thing, or if you can't, don't. Accepting has none of the passiveness of tolerance. Accepting is an active mode, the glad receiving of a present , a gift."

"Sir, I think I understand, but I also think that you exaggerate slightly. In small things ~ in everyday life ~ when things are not right, one simply wouldn't have the time or the energy to address them all. It would not be helpful, surely?"

"I am not talking of small things.", was Toy's immediate response. "And I am not talking of things that are 'not right'. I am talking of things that are wrong. Do you see the difference?"

No, Jones didn't see. It was too big a helping of received wisdom stood on its head to be digested in one meal; and he said so. Toy acknowledged the frank admission with a slight inclination of his head.

"The man who has Zen makes perfect shots, even with a billiard cue."

Whether this meant that a man so blessed could effectively use a cue as a golf club, or whether he was automatically an ace snooker player was not made clear.

"Play tomorrow morning. Take Mary with you. We'll see how you get on."

❋   ❋

Driving home, Jones still felt a bit shaky. It had been a hard lesson, and only his unswerving faith in the Old Man's integrity had kept him steady to his course.

But where *was* the lesson? Clearly he had a long way to go yet, if he could be so upset by something so trivial. That in itself, the realisation of brute ignorance in the face of wisdom was a kind of learning. Perhaps that was the lesson. No. It was the business of acceptance ~ true acceptance ~ that he was being taught. Very difficult, that and 'tolerance'.

Jones and The Girl
- A Diptych -
First Part

"The man who desires but acts not breeds pestilence...
Expect poison from the standing water."

William Blake.

10

The next day Jones deliberately drove the long way round to the golf course, following Tiger Brennan Drive. Mary noticed, and asked him why.

"Why? Because I want to have more time with you, that's why. There's nothing sinister about it; I just enjoy your company, that's all."

He was engagingly frank.

She laughed. "I enjoy your company too, but there's no need to be so devious. After the game we can drive out to Humpty Doo, if you like, and I'll introduce you to my friend Nelly.

"Uncle is going out for lunch", she added, by way of explanation.

Jones played like a man inspired, having another good round ~ in spite of the new putter. The Old Man was quite right, he could make just as many poor shots with an ordinary club as he ever could with his precious 'tool'.

Mary followed discretely, a mobile dappled shadow in the glaring sunlight, turning a few heads but, as before, not provoking the kind of interest one might have expected. She seemed to glide rather than walk and when stationary, demonstrated a rock-like immobility that granted her the ability to merge with the background. Five foot ten in her plimsolls, thin as a lath, and dressed in sky-blue shirt and trousers she could easily be mistaken for a boy. At a distance.

On the drive to Humpty Doo, closeted in the air-conditioned comfort of the car ~ and helped, no doubt, by the illicit atmosphere of truancy ~ Jones discovered that, amazingly, they had more in common than he could ever have guessed at. Real things, things that mattered.

As the miles of never-changing bush slid by the windows, the conversation flew back and forth like a shuttlecock, a kaleidoscope of ideas and information, the topics varied and far-ranging. Rarely had he felt so at ease in another's company and clearly it was not just one-sided.

Inevitably, they touched on intimacies ~

"What does you wife think of golf?"

"I no longer have a wife."

"Oh!" Her hand flew to her mouth in a pretty gesture of contrition. "I'm sorry..."

"Don't be." Jones remained po-faced. "There's nothing dramatic. As soon as the boys had lives of their own she divorced me. Simple as that."

It was impossible to read the rapid flux of expressions that raced across the other's features.

"And yourself?" Jones took the silence as an opening. "Are you married?" There was no ring on her finger.

She smiled, a faint wistful smile. "No. But I should be."

"You should be! Whatever do you mean?"

Did she blush? It would be difficult to tell with half her face already stained crimson.

"I'm going to have a baby", she said. "I have known for three months now."

"Good heavens!" Jones was both shocked and astonished. "I'd never had guessed, not in a million years!"

"No, it doesn't show, not yet. But there is no doubt. I have seen her ~ it is a 'her' ~ on a television screen at the hospital."

It seemed both pointless and impolite to enquire about the father.

And Jones didn't want to know anything about him, this ~ this usurper. But he had to be certain:

"There's no chance, I suppose, that the father..." he let the sentence trail away unfinished.

"No."

It was all he needed.

Jones and The Girl
- Second Part -

*"You don't look different
But you have changed,
I'm looking through you
You're not the same."*

The Beatles ~ Pop Song.

11

Humpty Doo (pop 1265) is a one-horse outback settlement not far from Darwin which, sadly, offers nothing of interest other than its name. Jones had driven through it often enough (blink and you'd miss it) never giving the place a moment's thought ~ beyond wondering what it was that could possibly induce people to live there, in this sun-blasted desolation.

A partial answer, courtesy of Mary, was to be found at the end of a mile-long dirt track which ended abruptly at a fenced-in compound. A young Abbo stood at the opened gate grinning like a monkey ~ the car's red dust cloud having smoke-signalled their coming.

"Hi! Charlie. How's things?"

"Good, Missy! Good!"

Jones drove through and waited, to give the boy a lift. Charlie padlocked the gate behind them and then, astonishingly, sprinted past the car, head thrown back, arms going like pistons. He beat them to the house by a whisker.

"Boss not here, Missy. Gone to town." The boy spoke staccato, between great gulps of air.

"Oh, Charlie! You should have said so at the gate. You *are* naughty." (This stern rebuke was received by Charlie with an almost apoplectic pleasure).

"Never mind, it doesn't really matter, it's Nelly we've come to see."

It was then that the strange episode occurred.

It was hot, fiendishly hot, standing out there in the open ~ without a hat ~ the unshaded temperature creeping up into the hundred-and-tens. The air was like molten glass, thick and viscous; the landscape trembled in the heat-haze. Jones felt faint.

The scenario: Charlie stands to Jones' left, his dirty vest glowing an unhealthy-looking green. Directly ahead, the girl, a piebald vertical slash, and, behind her ~ emerging from the shadow of the house ~ a huge alien 'thing', six feet tall, its long neck jerking rhythmically as it picked its way towards them, high-stepping on great clawed feet.

For a long moment the scene was freeze-framed, with everything rendered in sharp exquisite detail ~ but a scene completely devoid of meaning ~ surreal ~ a challenge to the senses.

Then, slowly, the characters gradually came back to life, back to real-life mummery: the boy, the girl, the emu. No one had noticed the strange transition, or Jones' discomfort. Mary was talking (he could hear her now) as if nothing out of the way had happened; as if, for a few seconds the world had not wobbled on its axis.

The travesty of a bird nuzzled its beak against Mary's hip, its eyes gleaming wickedly, darting to and fro, expecting a caress or a titbit. So, this was her friend, a creature as bizarre as her natural self. Yet it made a kind of sense, this alliance of outsiders from beyond the norm. Heaven only knew what kind of oddity the errant Boss would have provided...

Having been tickled under the chin and with nothing more substantial in the offing, Nelly wandered off, leaving the surreal tableau to the trio of quasi-humans.

Later, Jones was to mark this moment as the major turning point of his life ~ the key that turned in his lock. For the present, though, in the precious seconds that still remained before mundane normality returned, Jones, not fully conscious of what he was doing ~ yet aware of the necessity for doing it ~ reached out and touched Mary's face, tracing the contours of Africa with his fingertips. She did not pull away.

There was a communion between them.

"To be awakened at all is to be awakened completely,
for, having no parts or divisions
the Buddha-nature is not realised bit by bit."

Lin-Chi (d 876).

12

"Well, how's the golf?"

Toy's face gave nothing away. Did he know about Mary? It seemed hardly likely that she'd tell him...

"The golf goes well, Sir. I will be in need of a new handicap if this continues."

"If?"

Yes, Toy did know. What other reason could there be for him to even suggest that he might not continue.

"I meant, Sir, that if my game stays at its present level, or if it impr..."

"If!" Toy interrupted him. "There you go again ~ if, if. You are full of doubt, full of fear. Once it was doubt that you might not improve, and now it is fear that your improvement will not be maintained. What a sorry man you are. I pity any poor girl who marries you ~ such a doubter! You would poison her with your own disbelieving."

So, Toy not only knew, he was warning him off! Abashed, Jones sat silent, head down, hoping to hide the semaphore-signals of his face.

Toy did not let him hide for long.

"Listen! Head up when I speak to you. Show respect even if you do not feel it." Toy was sharp with him.

"That's better. Now, you came here ~ you say ~ to improve your golf. Let us see if we can move in that direction."

Jones was all attention.

"What do you have in your mind when you address the ball?"

Jones thought.

"I concentrate hard Sir, with all my will. I picture the ball flying to the pin. Only a successful shot is in my mind."

"Positive thinking, would you say?"

"Yes, exactly that. Positive thinking. I remove all thoughts of failure."

"Does it work, this thinking positively? Does it give results?"

A good question.

. "No, not all the time ~ not very often, actually." A pause. "But I imagine that if I didn't even think I'd make a good shot, I'd be ten times worse."

"Do you now."

Toy lit another cigarette and indulged himself in a little gentle parody, speaking out of the corner of his mouth, the cigarette still in place.

"I will hit the ball squarely. It will fly to the mark. Yes? If I only think it hard enough and long enough then ~" Bang! Toy smacked the table hard, making Jones jump ~ "then the thought will become actuality. Have you ever heard such rubbish! No wonder you're only a twelve handicap. What else could you expect from a man who fills his head with such tosh."

He removed the cigarette from his mouth and tapped off the ash.

"Let us examine this positive thinking of yours. It is highly valued in the West, I believe, so highly valued in fact, that to question it might be considered close to sacrilegious. Well, I am going to offer you an opportunity for heresy."

Jones sat open-mouthed. The Old Man was in earnest, deadly earnest. His seriousness was palpable. But it was absurd! How could positive thinking not be beneficial?

"You think it absurd? My questioning your received wisdom, your shibboleth? But why not? Anything that's worth the candle can withstand a little scrutiny, and you never know, you might even learn something."

This all came as something of a surprise, not to say a shock, to Jones. He simply couldn't believe it.

"But Sir, this means that you're advocating negative thinking. How can that be? It makes no sense... Am I expected to think that my swing is going to go wide, or that I might even slice the ball! How is that ever going to help my game?"

Toy was entirely unmoved,

"No, not negative thinking; that's no help either. You see only opposites. You cannot see that between the two extremes there is a middle way."

Jones did not look convinced.

"Look, all cherries are fruit, aren't they?" Toy asked.

Jones agreed that they were.

"But all fruits are not cherries. Think on it."

Jones thought on it. And got no further.

The Chinaman persevered:

"Let us imagine that you have a difficulty, an insoluble problem." Clearly he was no longer talking about fruit. "This problem will not yield. It will not yield to that which you already know, to what you can bring to it from your store of knowledge and experience.

"Positive thinking, by its nature, only dwells in the realm of what is already known ~ and this has been shown to be insufficient. No, what is required is new material, information from the as yet unknown. In short, creative thinking; a creative solution is required, not the eternal juggling of what's already in your head. Creative for you, I might add, even though the solution might well be a commonplace to others."

It was getting late. Shadows were gathering in the corners of the room. Toy did not need to look at his clocks.

"I am growing tired", he said. "Entering unknown territory ~ being creative ~ is a high-risk business. Yet one must plunge in, eyes open or shut ~ but plunge! not falter on the brink. Dipping in a toe to test the water will never make a fish of you.

"So, do not fill your mind with rose-tinted visions of happy expectations. Empty your mind of dross.

"That's enough for today. We have dealt with the so-called wisdom of the West, tomorrow we must look at the East, and see what that has to offer."

Third Interlude

"To me, Zen is intellectual quicksand ~ anarchy, darkness, meaninglessness, chaos.
It is tantalizing and infuriating.
And yet it is humourous, refreshing, enticing.
"... One of the basic tenets of Zen Buddhism is that there is no way to characterise what Zen is.
"... It might seem, then, that all efforts to explain Zen are complete wastes of time.
But that is not the attitude of Zen masters and students."

Douglas R. Hofstadter: 'Gödel, Escher, Bach'.

The Japanese word Zen ~ Ch'en in Chinese ~ means meditation.

A very brief history of Zen

Tradition has it that Zen first came to China with the arrival in 520 of the Indian monk Bodhidarma. But it is clear that many of Zen's key concepts were already in place, in China, long before then. For instance, Zen can not claim a patent on 'having nothing to say'.

"*Those who know do not speak,*
Those who speak do not know."

These immortal lines are from Lao-tzu, and date from the fifth century ~ BC.

In brief, Zen, or more properly, Zen Buddhism, is a blend of Chinese Taoism and Indian Mahayana Buddhism. The process of assimilation was both long and gradual with many schisms, deviations and swings of emphasis between the Buddhist and Taoist elements.

However, the beginnings of a truly Chinese Zen are marked by the life and teaching of Hui-neng (637-713). This remarkable man ~ an illiterate peasant from Canton ~ had his first awakening when, as a boy, he overheard someone reciting from a Buddhist text, the Vajracchedika.

In this text are the profound but obscure words of Buddha:

"I obtained not the least thing from un-excelled, complete awakening, and for this very reason it is called un-excelled complete awakening."

Through Hui-neng and his followers, Zen flourished mightily during the last two hundred years of the T'ang dynasty (about 700-900) and, in a sense, was a victim of its own success. The tenth and eleventh centuries were particularly fruitful, bringing great prosperity to Zen's door. Literally. Parents sent their children to Zen masters for an education and, almost overnight, the relatively small communities of dedicated scholars were transformed into the equivalent of boys' boarding schools.

To accommodate this huge influx ~ and to keep order ~ sitting meditation (za-zen) and koans (seemingly unanswerable questions) were introduced ~ along with liberal application of the stick.

No doubt sitting in silence for hours on end is a useful tool when having to deal with large numbers of unruly boys, but ~ and it's a big 'but' ~ until this surge of popularity, there is no reference, anywhere, to the importance of meditation. Quite the contrary in fact: during the first five hundred years of Zen, what references there are to meditation are pejorative ones. For instance, here is Huai-jang addressing Ma-tsu:

> *"What is the objective of meditation?" asked Huai-jang.*
> *"To become a Buddha, answered Ma-Tsu.*

Huai-jang then picked up a floor tile and began to polish it on a rock.

> *"What are you doing master?" asked Ma-tsu.*
> *"I am polishing it for a mirror", said Huai-jang.*
> *"How could polishing a tile make a mirror?"*
> *"How could sitting in meditation make a Buddha?"*

There are several references to the idea that prolonged sitting is not much better than being dead. There is of course, a proper place for sitting ~ along with standing, walking and lying ~ but to imagine that sitting contains some special virtue is 'attachment to form'. Here is Hui-jang (a disciple of the great Hui-neng) once again:

"To train yourself in sitting meditation is to train yourself to be a sitting Buddha... You should know that Zen is neither sitting or lying... If you make yourself a sitting Buddha this is precisely killing the Buddha. If you adhere to the sitting position, you will not obtain the principle of Zen."

Zen continued to thrive in China until 1650 but it was in Japan that it survived and flourished. And despite the teaching of the Old Masters it was two variants of za-zen that were successfully exported in about 1200. Both the Rinzai and Soto schools are firmly based on sitting meditation and, in this form, Zen is once again in danger of becoming universally popular.

(For the most part taken from Allen Watt's *The Way of Zen*).

Daibai asked Baso: "What is Buddha?"
Baso said: "This mind is Buddha."

Mumon.

A monk asked Baso: "What is Buddha?
Baso said: "This mind is not Buddha."
"If anyone understands this he is a graduate of Zen."

Mumon.

13

The wisdom of the East!

Jones, still a fool, was almost beside himself with excitement. At last, the secret was about to be revealed. As he walked up the concrete stairway to Toy's apartment he could feel that it was going to be special day and, with a thrill of fear, he could also sense that this visit might very well be the last.

His premonition seemed borne out: the change in Toy's room was almost as shocking as the first glimpse of his great-granddaughter's face. The Old Man was sitting in the wrong chair! Jones set himself down gingerly, in Toy's vacated seat. It didn't feel right; and the view was all wrong.

Toy laughed.

"You should see your face. What a picture! Incredulity, pop-eyed horror, all dancing there in your features. Wonderful! Quite wonderful. How expressive the face is."

"But why? Why change seats?" Jones asked.

"Why? Because we are going to change roles, that's why. Have you never heard of Fritz Perls and his gestalt chair-changing? No? Never mind. Today I ask the questions and you will give the answers."

Jones made no reply to this. He didn't feel at all comfortable ~ which was no doubt part of Toy's intention.

"So, Mr. Jones, tell me about the wisdom of the East."

"But I've come here for you to tell me", Jones blustered. "I don't know what it is. I wouldn't be here if I did."

"Wouldn't you?"

There was the suspicion of a twinkle behind the Old Man's spectacle lenses.

Again, Toy had unerringly hit the mark: Mary. This quietened Jones somewhat, and he settled back in the master's chair to seriously consider the question.

"The wisdom of the East. Well, I don't know, but I'd guess that somewhere, somehow, meditation comes into it."

"Go on."

"I can't go on. I don't even know how to meditate properly; at least, I don't think I do. I was rather hoping that you'd be giving me some instruction."

Being the 'pupil' didn't stop Toy from lighting-up one of his Winfields.

"Why do you meditate", he asked.

Jones thought for a moment.

"To free my mind, to liberate myself."

"You wish to be free? Is that it?"

"Yes."

"Who is this person that so constrains you that you yearn for freedom?"

A pause.

"There is no such person."

"No?"

A longer pause. "

Yes", Jones said. "I constrain myself."

"Good. We're getting somewhere. Let's start again."

TOY: What is your aim when you meditate?

JONES: To still my mind. To quiet the dog-eat-tail of my racing thoughts.

TOY: They sound like someone else's words. Use your own.

JONES: (Chastened) I empty my mind.

TOY: That's more like it. Now, what is in your mind when you have emptied it?

JONES: Nothing. There is a void waiting to be filled.

TOY: Filled by what, pray?

JONES: By the Buddha-nature, by Awakening.

TOY: And does this happen? Does your empty mind awaken?

JONES: No Sir, it doesn't. But I persevered in the faith that eventually it will.

TOY: This sounds suspiciously like positive thinking to me: continuing a fruitless practice in the hope that one day everything will magically be made clear. Don't you agree?

JONES: Yes.

TOY: Well, it looks as though the wisdom of the East is no better founded than that of the West. No?

JONES: (reluctantly). Yes.

So, in the end, it had all come down to this. Nothing. There was nothing special for him to do, no exercises ~ spiritual or physical ~ no concentrative powers to tap, no focussing of attention, no mind-control. No anything. It was hugely disappointing and it showed.

"This is a hard lesson Sir ~ that there are no lessons, that there is nothing I can do to improve my game."

Toy did not seem in the least bit put out by his pupil's long face and depressive gloom. On the contrary, he looked positively cheerful in the face of his apparent failure.

"At last! You are learning."

Jones was startled.

"Learning? Am I?"

"Yes, you have learned ~ not just been told ~ you have learned that there is nothing special about Zen, that there is nothing special to seek. No great door-opening secret. The door is always open and always has been; it is you, with your seeking that have blocked the path. Now, knowing this, your progress will be un-hindered.

"But", he went on, "a man with an empty mind is no better than a block of wood. It is important that we distinguish between the vacuity of 'nothing' and the wisdom of holding to no-thing, or, if you prefer, nothing special, nothing in particular.

"Just be. Just enjoy your golf, enjoy your life, your ordinary, everyday life ~ seeking nothing ~ let this be your meditation. Swim in the nourishing soup of God's perfect world.

It was the 'soup' that did it. Of a sudden, Jones felt the soup. There was a great fractal blossoming of understanding ~ a brief dizzying wave that reached a glorious crescendo ~ then faded and died away...

Jones was awakened.

"There is no place in Buddhism for using effort. Just be ordinary and nothing special."

Lin-Chi (d.867).

*"Mediocrity is gone. Mind is clear of limitation.
I seek no state of enlightenment."*

Zen Flesh, Zen Bones.

14

... Strange, there was a different clock on the wall. Where was the hideous sunburst? Click! In a flash Jones was back, back in the familiar room, but seen from a different view-point. Toy was speaking to him:

"Mr. Jones, your desire to excel at golf ~ which brought you here ~ is an expression of your desire to excel in life, to live fully. To truly feel.

"Sir", he continued, "I pronounce you a free man. Go and play your golf ~ un-hindered ~ secure in the knowledge that improving one's game is more than just a matter of taking less shots at a golf ball.

"Why should a monk live alone,
without the comfort and company of a woman?
The need for both is eternal,
fixed in the blood and bone ~
why then deny it?
Why deny that particular aspect of God's bounty?
To avoid distraction...
Distraction from what?
From one's own selfish wish for Enlightenment,
that's what.
It seems a strange sort of contract;
you can not bargain with the ocean."

The Seventh Patriarch.

15

A week later, Jones was back ~ figuratively speaking ~ with cap in hand.

"Sir, I wish to speak to you as Mary's great-grandfather."

"Yes."

"Yesterday, I changed my given name from John to Joseph."

"Aah!" Toy's face lit up. "I follow you. Before or after?"

"Before."

"Good. You make this old man very happy. Your obligation is discharged, the temple has been built. Thank you.

"But", he added, almost as an afterthought, "will she make you a good wife?"

Jones looked him square in the eye. "Does a dog have Buddha-nature?" he asked.

Toy smiled with his whole face, an alarming corrugation of lines and wrinkles.

"Welcome, son."

"Welcome, father."

"Has a dog Buddha-nature?
This is the most serious question of all.
If you say yes or no,
You lose your own Buddha-nature. "

Mumon *'The Gateless Gate.'*

- Postscript -

"It is no small thing to overcome the accident of one's birth."

After St. Augustine.

16

"Are you sure you're pregnant ~ there's no sign of it."

But the black stubble that burned under his finger-tips told sufficient of a story. It was the clear evidence of the ultra-scan's requirements and not a half-hearted attempt to ape the schoolgirl.

Yet that was exactly what she looked like: a great big schoolgirl, lying on his bed, gawky, angular, ribs and bones showing clearly beneath transparent yellow skin.

"Why are you so tall?" he asked her.

"My mother was a Dutch woman."

Jones noted the 'was' and left it alone.

"I see...You know, you really are very beautiful."

The compliment was sincerely meant and not intended as a morale-booster.

A pause to summon up his courage.

"Have you had many lovers?"

It was a foolish question, but a question that every lover asks, in the vain hope that if not the first, then they are at least one of an elite. And surely, in Mary's case, most men would be repelled rather than attracted by the punctuation of her face.

"Oh yes, many."

She laughed, a genuine happy sound and turned towards him, propping herself on one bony elbow, the black bell of her hair set swinging.

"Yes, many men have loved me."

She glanced quickly at his face.

"You look surprised."

"Yes, I ~", then the penny dropped.

"Of course! Your face, your birthmark. You carry it with such ~ such grace ~ that it becomes a kind of badge. With you it's not an impediment at all! It's a lure and I'm just another silly fish that's been caught on your hook."

"No", she said, "not just another. You are very special ~ I chose you."

She leaned over him, the strawberry face close to his own.

"Lie still", she hissed. "I'm going to ride you."

❉   ❉

Darkness comes quickly in the tropics. The light had drained from the room, acting as a kindness, hiding away the absence of all the trivia by which a man attempts to lay the ghost of a room's previous inhabitants and to invest the place, temporarily, with a little of himself.

He had, he thought, been unencumbered by people or possessions and, until now, had never felt the lack; never sensed the emptiness of his room, or of his life. He had been nothing more than a stranger in a strange land, just passing through; one of St. Augustine's *civitas peregrina*, a resident stranger. But now he wanted, with a great want, to be attached once more to the world of men.

It was not that this sensation was new to Jones, far from it. It was just that it had been such a long time ~ since he had last felt it ~ that he'd never expected the sensation to visit him again.

It was heady, intoxicating stuff. Thrilling to a degree, and he told her so.

"Better than golf?" she whispered, a great wicked smiling face hovering, unseen, above him.

"No, not better..." he paused, his timing perfect, ..."but just as good."

In the darkness there was the sound of a hand, clapping.

"The smell of Zen"...
I like that.

The Seventh Patriarch

- *Acknowledgments* -

'*The Way of Zen*' by Allan Watts and the Shambala Pocket Classic '*Zen Flesh, Zen Bones*', have both proved indispensable in writing this book. However, the interpretation of Zen is entirely my own and is in no way attributable to or reflected by the authors of the two aforementioned excellent works.

With regard to the Seventh Patriarch: In eighth century China, when Hui-neng, the Sixth Patriarch died, the office of Patriarch died with him.

As far as I know, there actually is a Jimmy Ah Toy. He lends his name to the big corrugated iron shed that acts as Pine Creek's general store and post-office. I have never met him. This book is dedicated to the memory of his father, the remarkably intrepid Jimmy Ah You, who, if he did not have Zen, must have had something very much like it.

Cromer
N. Norfolk
Spring 1997